GUMBRELLA

BARRY ROOT

G. P. Putnam's Sons
New York

For Janna

G. P. Putnam's Sons, Reg. U.S. Pat. & Tm. Off. Published simultaneously in Canada.
Printed in Hong Kong by South China Printing Co. (1988) Ltd.
Designed by Gunta Alexander. Text set in Maiandra.
The artwork was done in watercolor, gouache, and pastel pencil on 140 lb. Arches Hot Press paper.

Library of Congress Cataloging-in-Publication Data
Root, Barry. Gumbrella / Barry Root. p. cm. Summary: Gumbrella loves nursing sick animals back to
health, but she hates letting them go. [1. Animal rescue—Fiction. 2. Animals—Fiction.]
I. Title. PZ7.R6775 Gu 2002 [E]—dc21 00-068406 ISBN 0-399-23347-4
1 3 5 7 9 10 8 6 4 2
First Impression

Gumbrella was a good little elephant, and believed in helping her fellow animals if she could, especially the cute ones. So when Trumbull, her brother, brought home an injured mouse, she knew exactly what to do.

"We'll start an animal hospital!" she told Trumbull. "I'll be the nurse."

"And I'll be the doctor!" said Trumbull.

"No, I'm the nurse AND the doctor. You can be the ambulance," said Gumbrella. She scooped up her first patient, whose name was Eric, and took him inside.

Gumbrella couldn't wait to get started.

She made a splint
for Eric's leg
out of toothpicks
and a Band-Aid.

She brought him
his meals on a tray,
just like in a real hospital.

She bathed him and petted him.

She read to him and made get-well cards for him
and checked on him at least every five minutes.

After a few days, Eric was feeling better and wanted to go home.

"Go home! What a ridiculous idea!" said Gumbrella.

She took his pulse. "Uh-oh!"

She checked his blood pressure. "Oh, dear!"

She took his temperature. "My goodness! It's worse than I thought!" she said.

Eric decided maybe he didn't feel so well after all.

Gumbrella sent her brother out to look for more patients.
Trumbull tromped off into the woods and came back
an hour later with a sick bird—a warbler with laryngitis.

"Poor little darling thing!" cried Gumbrella, and she mixed
up some hot salty water and made the bird gargle.

After a week or so, the bird's throat had cleared up
and she and Eric were feeling fine.

"When will we be going home?" they asked.

"It's too soon to even think of it!" said Gumbrella,
who was already planning next month's menu.

Winter came in with a roar, giving Trumbull plenty to do.
He found squirrels with sniffles, mice with measles and moles
with mumps. He brought them all inside and went out to find
more. There were crows with croup, rabbits with rashes,
an owl with a migraine and a groundhog who just wanted
to go back to sleep.

More patients meant more work, but that was no problem for Gumbrella. "Everyone into bed!" she ordered, and before the animals could say "Hello," they found themselves tucked in under piles of blankets with comfortable pillows.

"I think we're all feeling a lot better now," said Eric one day.
"Don't you think it's time we were going home?"

"Oh, no, you're still far too weak to be out in those cold
woods by yourselves," said Gumbrella, who didn't want them
to leave before she finished sewing hospital gowns for them.

The days grew longer and the weather warmer.
The animals were becoming truly restless. Even
the groundhog was wide awake and dying to get outside.

"What about today?" asked an upstart otter one
beautiful spring morning.

"Yes, what about today?" cried the groundhog.

"Today, today!" cried all the animals. "We want
to go home today!"

"No, not today," said Gumbrella, who was planning
the program for the evening.

The animals had seen better dancing, but they all sat
through it and clapped politely. All of them, that is, except
Eric. Eric had had enough. Besides, he had seen where
Gumbrella kept the key to the back door.

Gumbrella finished her last dance and did a long, low bow. The applause sounded different this time, more like wings flapping and feet scurrying. When she looked up, the animals were gone!

Gumbrella was so upset that she locked herself in her room
and refused to eat anything except dessert. She left Trumbull a note
saying that she had come down with a rare type of laryngitis
that could only be cured if the animals came back.

Trumbull was very concerned.

The animals were sorry to hear that Gumbrella was unwell,
and they wanted to help. "Gumbrella took us in and looked after us
when we needed it. We should do the same for her," they said.
So they made a stretcher out of sticks and hurried back
to the house with Trumbull.

Gumbrella was delighted to see the animals.
She wasn't so sure about the stretcher.
"But *I'm* the doctor," she kept saying in a tiny voice.
"Not today!" said Eric.

The animals took good care of Gumbrella.
They bathed her and fed her and petted her
and sang to her and took her temperature
every five minutes.

"I think I'm feeling better now. When can I
go home?" Gumbrella asked.

"It's too soon to even think of it!" they told her.

They knew just the right way to take care of a patient.
They had learned from Gumbrella herself.